Hide and Snake

Keith Baker

A TRUMPET CLUB SPECIAL EDITION

Published by The Trumpet Club
666 Fifth Avenue, New York, New York 10103

ISBN 0-440-84980-2

This edition published by arrangement with Harcourt
Brace Jovanovich, Inc.

Printed in the United States of America
February 1993

The illustrations in this book were done in Liquitex
acrylics on illustration board.
The display type was set in ITC Zapf International
Medium Italic.
The text type was set in Zapf International Medium.
Composition by Thompson Type, San Diego,
California.
Designed by Michael Farmer

10 9 8 7 6 5 4 3 2 1
DAN

Friends—
I'll see you around—
and over and under and
through ....

Keith Baker

1993

Ready or not—here I go!

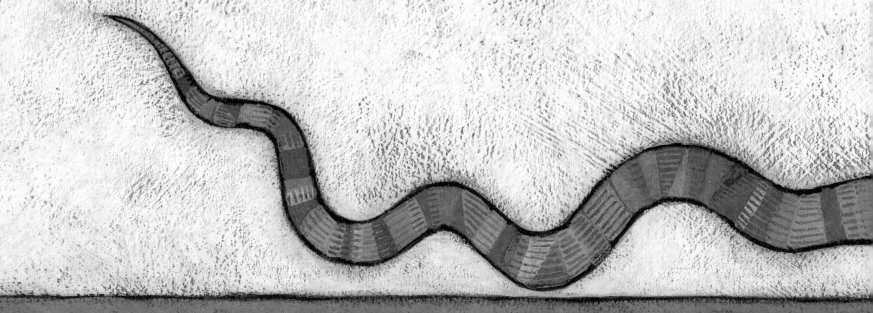

I'm looping through yarn,

curling 'round hats,

wrapping 'round presents,

and napping with cats.

I'm frosting the cakes,

ticking with clocks,

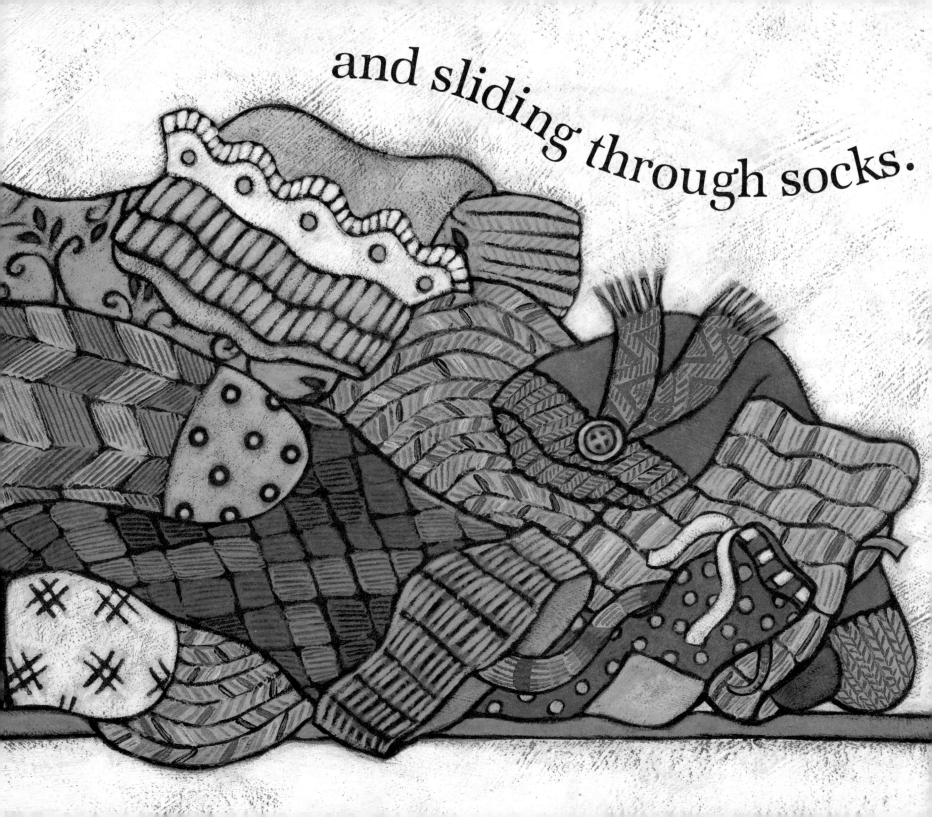

and sliding through socks.

I'm playing with toys,

twisting 'round vases,

weaving through baskets,

and tangling with laces.

I'm hiding from you —

in so many places!

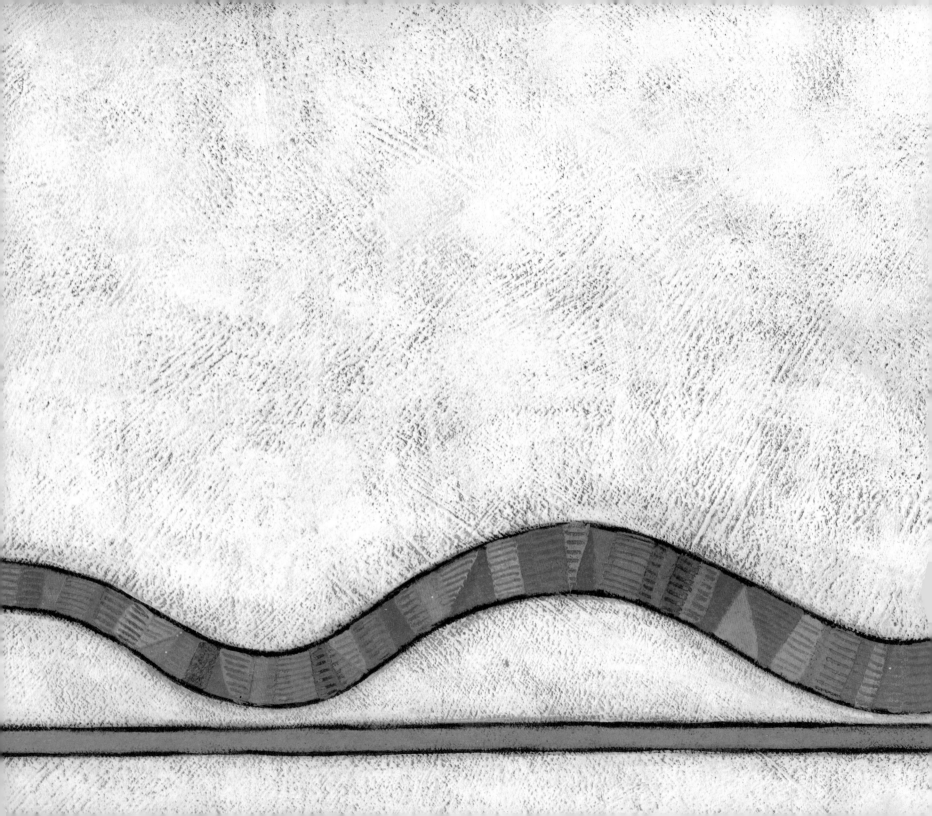